ELMER and the RACE

David McKee

Andersen Press

Elmer, the patchwork elephant, was walking with his cousin, Wilbur, when a group of noisy young elephants came charging past.
"What's going on?" Elmer asked.
"We were seeing who is the fastest," said one, "and it was me."
"It wasn't, it was me!" said another.

"When the immortal scorer
writes against your name,
he'll write not if you won or lost
but how you played the game."

– a misquote of Grantland Rice

First published in Great Britain in 2016 by Andersen Press Ltd.,
20 Vauxhall Bridge Road, London SW1V 2SA.

Colour separated in Switzerland by Photolitho AG, Zürich.
Printed and bound in China.

1 3 5 7 9 10 8 6 4 2

British Library Cataloguing in Publication Data available.

ISBN 978 1 78344 417 5 (hardback)
ISBN 978 1 78344 455 7 (paperback)

"You both cheated," said a third. "It wasn't a proper race."

"Let's have a proper race," said Wilbur.

"We need to tell the other animals and decide the course," said Elmer. "We'll have the race next week."

It was a busy, noisy week. The other animals promised to come and watch. There was always one or other of the young elephants practising and older elephants cheering them on.

On the day, nine elephants turned up to race.
Each racer was decorated a different colour.

Blue moaned about being blue so Red agreed to swap with him. Finally they were ready.

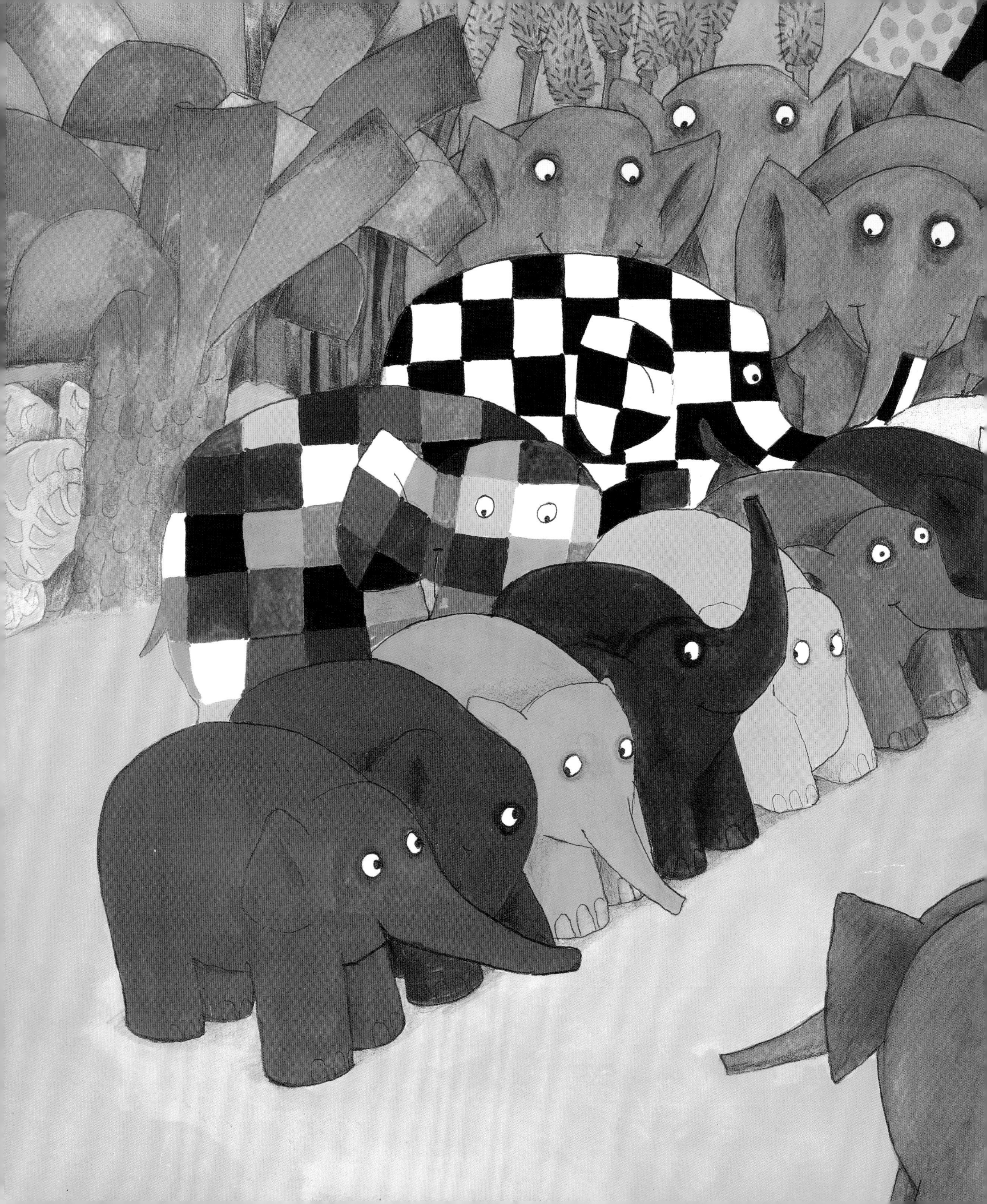

"Good luck," said Elmer. "Remember it's not just who is fastest or slowest, but how you run the race. READY!" he called.

"STEADY!" said Wilbur.

"GO!" they shouted together, and the racers were off.

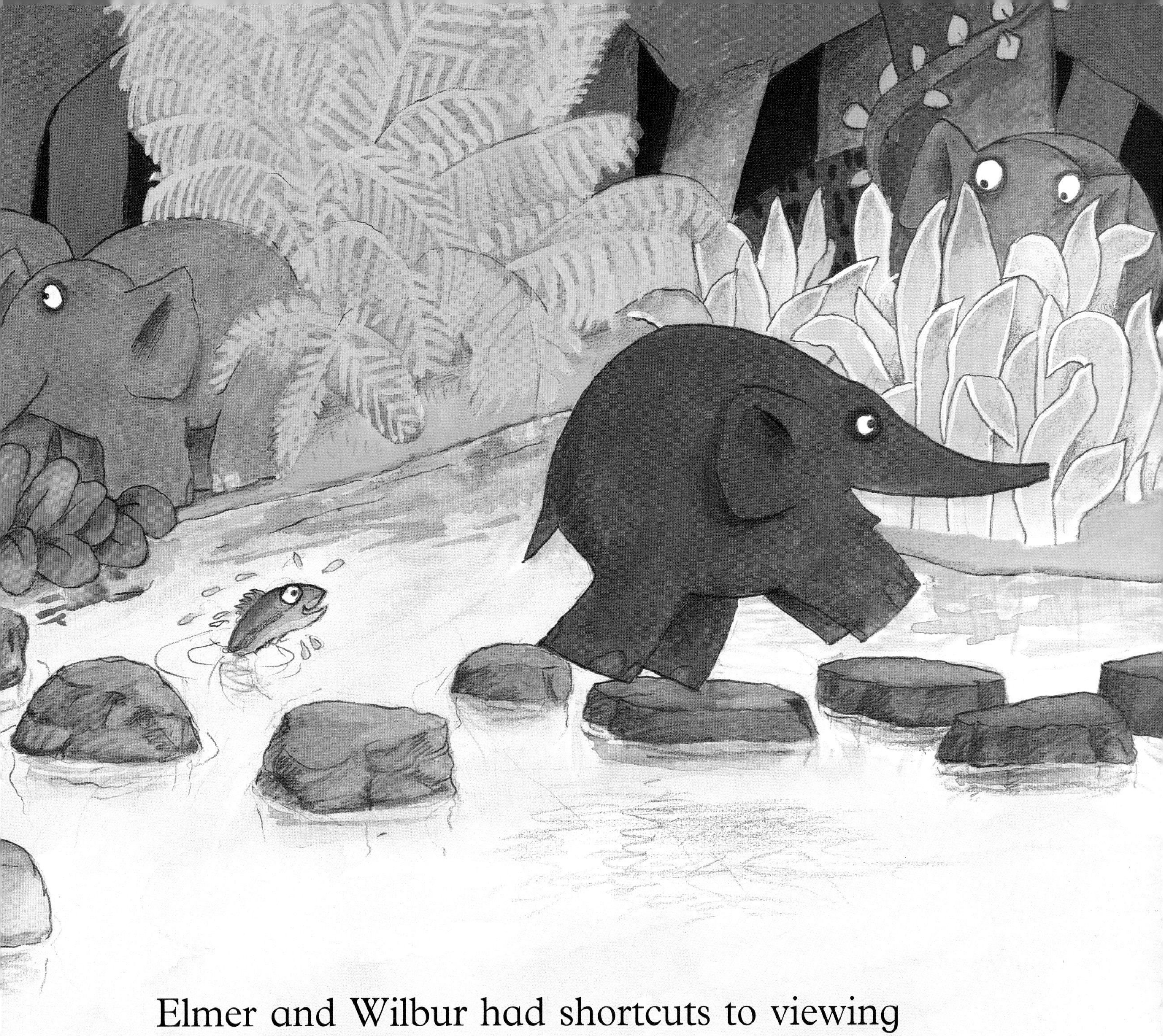

Elmer and Wilbur had shortcuts to viewing places along the route. The first was the river, where Brown was well ahead of the others. The crocodiles cheered.
"Brown has started fastest," said Wilbur.
"There's still a long way to go," said Elmer.

Next it was Monkey Corner. The cheeky monkeys confused the racers by throwing fruit and shouting, “That way!” “No, this way!”

“Faster! Faster! Turn here!”
Pink and Violet went off in the wrong direction while the others caught up with Brown.

After that there was a hill.
At the top Yellow was ahead
with Green close behind.
“Pink and Violet are still lost,”
chuckled Elmer.

At Red Rock Pass, Yellow deliberately tripped
Green as she tried to overtake.
“Cheat! Cheat!” roared Lion and Tiger.
Green was hurt and White stopped to help her.
“Lucky we saw that,” said Wilbur.

Elmer and Wilbur reached the last viewing place just as Orange prepared to pass Yellow. Yellow was ready to trip him up, as he had Green.
"BOO!" shouted the hippos. Blue saw his chance and passed them both.
"Yellow is disqualified," said Elmer.

Blue stayed ahead and won.
"That would be me if I hadn't changed colour," said Red.
Pink and Violet arrived together, laughing too much to run.

Last was injured Green with White helping her.
Yellow was ashamed and went to say sorry.
"Now for the medals," said Wilbur.

“Well,” said Elmer, “Blue gets the medal for finishing first and Orange for finishing second (without a second you can’t have a first). There are also medals for the fastest starter, the bravest, the kindest and the unluckiest. There are two for funniest and one for the sorriest, who used to be the naughtiest. Another day we might have another story. Three cheers for all of you.”